Please return / renew by d
You can renew it at:
norlink.norfolk.gov.uk

FISHES' CLAWS
AND
DINOSAURS' PAWS

Seriously Silly Stories

by
Adam Bushnell

Illustrated by Vince Reid

First Published
April 2009 in Great Britain by

PUBLISHING

© **Adam Bushnell 2009**

All rights reserved. No part of this publication may be reproduced in any
form or by any means without the written permission of the publisher

The moral right of the author has been asserted in accordance with the
Copyright, Designs and Patents Act 1988

A CIP record for this work is available from the British Library

ISBN-10: 1-905637-76-4
ISBN-13: 978-1-905637-76-8

Typeset by Educational Printing Services Limited

Educational Printing Services Limited

E-mail: enquiries@eprint.co.uk   Website: www.eprint.co.uk

Contents

1: Anansi and the Corn
(Caribbean)

Anansi the spider loved corn on the cob and sweetcorn. It was his favourite food!

One day, he said to his friends Monkey and Tiger, "I love corn on the cob so much that I think we should plant our own corn in the field and grow as much as we want. We could share it between the three of us."

1

Monkey and Tiger agreed, so they spent the rest of the day planting the corn seeds in the ground.

Eventually the corn grew big and strong but when Anansi, Monkey and Tiger arrived at the corn field they saw that someone had been stealing the corn; there was lots of it missing!

Monkey was angry.

Tiger was even angrier.

But Anansi, he was so angry that Monkey and Tiger thought he was going to explode.

"Hey," whispered Monkey to Tiger,

"Anansi seems a little bit too angry about the corn. You don't think it was him that stole it, do you?"

"There's only one way to find out," Tiger whispered back. "Tonight when it gets dark we'll hide and catch the thief red-handed." So that night Monkey hid in the mango tree and Tiger hid in the long grass.

Sure enough, the thief arrived and started eating the corn.

Monkey jumped out of the tree.

Tiger leapt from the long grass.

They saw the thief . . . it was Anansi!

Monkey and Tiger began to chase after Anansi. The spider knew that he couldn't outrun his friends, so he said to a grain of corn on the ground, "Grain of corn, please hide me!"

The grain of corn opened up and Anansi climbed inside.

Monkey and Tiger ran straight past.

Just then Rooster woke up. As it was morning he crowed and started looking for his breakfast.

Rooster saw the grain of corn on the ground. He stepped up to it and SLURP! gobbled it up! He gobbled up the grain of corn that had Anansi inside.

Suddenly, Alligator climbed out of the river and started walking along the path looking for his breakfast. He saw Rooster, licked his lips and walked over to him. SNAP! Alligator gobbled up the cockerel. He gobbled up Rooster who had the grain of corn inside that had Anansi inside!

Meanwhile, Monkey and Tiger had been searching for Anansi everywhere. When they couldn't find him, they decided to go and see the great and mighty Oracle Drum. The Oracle Drum knew all things!

Tiger began to play the Oracle Drum and asked, "Where can we find Anansi?"

Oracle Drum replied, "Anansi is inside . . . Grain of corn . . . Grain of corn . . . Grain of corn . . . Grain of corn . . . Anansi is inside . . . Rooster . . . Rooster . . . Rooster . . . Rooster . . . Rooster . . . Rooster . . . Anansi is inside . . . Alligator . . . Alligator . . . Alligator . . . Alligator . . . Alligator . . ."

"Inside a grain of corn, inside Rooster, inside Alligator?!" exclaimed Tiger. "That sounds crazy! But Oracle Drum has never been wrong before. Let's go and see."

Monkey and Tiger went off searching for Anansi and after a while they found Alligator.

Tiger opened up Alligator's mouth and inside he found Rooster. So he opened up Rooster's beak and inside he found the grain of corn. He opened up the grain of corn . . . and out jumped Anansi!

Monkey and Tiger began to chase after Anansi. But the spider couldn't outrun his friends, so he said to the banana tree, "Banana tree, please hide me!"

The banana tree cast down one of its fibres and Anansi began to climb up it. When he got to the top, he pulled the fibre to him and threw it over to the mango tree nearest to the banana tree. Anansi climbed along the fibre and hung upside down between the two trees.

He then blew the biggest raspberry at
Monkey and Tiger that they had ever heard,

"TTTHHHHWWWWPPPPPPPPPPPP!!!!!!!!!"

Monkey and Tiger were furious! But
just then Tiger smiled and said, "Just a
moment, Anansi. We may be too big to climb
up onto that fibre after you BUT when
Monkey gets hungry, I can wait here while
he gets his lunch. When I get hungry,
Monkey can wait here while I get my lunch.

What will you do when you get hungry Anansi? If you climb down from there . . . we'll get you!"

Anansi got scared. His favourite food was corn on the cob and that grew on the ground!

The spider had an idea. He made a web from the fibres of the banana tree and from that day on he stopped eating corn on the cob and started eating . . . flies!

Eventually, Anansi did climb down from his web and he did make friends again with Monkey and Tiger – but that's another story.

2: Tchang's Quest
(Chinese)

Tchang lived with his mother on a farm in China. They lived simple lives and were happy enough, but no matter what they planted, nothing seemed to grow on their farm.

One day Tchang said to his mother, "I'm going to see the Great King of the

West, and ask him why nothing grows on our farm."

Tchang hugged his mother tightly and then set off walking.

He walked and walked and walked, for forty-nine days and forty-nine nights, until at last, breathless and panting, he came to a house. He knocked at the door.

KNOCK! KNOCK! KNOCK!

An old woman answered and said, "Why, hello there, dear. What can I do for you then?"

Tchang said, "I'm on my way to see the Great King of the West to ask him a question, but I was just wondering, perhaps, if I could spend the night at your place. I'm exhausted!"

The old woman smiled a toothless grin and said, "You're welcome to stay at my place, but would you mind asking the Great King of the West a question for me as well? Would you ask him why my daughter cannot speak?"

Tchang said, "I *promise* I'll ask your question."

He then spent that night sleeping soundly at the house and the next morning he set off walking.

He walked and walked and walked, for

forty-nine days and forty-nine nights, until at last, breathless and panting, he came to a farm. He knocked at the door.

KNOCK! KNOCK! KNOCK!

A farmer answered and said, "Hello! What can I do for you young man?"

Tchang said, "I'm on my way to see the Great King of the West to ask him a question, but I was just wondering, perhaps, if I could spend the night at your place. I'm exhausted!"

The farmer replied, "Oh you'd be welcome to spend the night here, but . . . um, could you ask him a question for me as well please? Could you ask him why my fruit trees grow no fruit?"

Tchang said, "I *promise* I'll ask your question."

The next morning he set off walking.

He walked and walked and walked, for forty-nine days and forty-nine nights, until at last, breathless and panting, he came to a river. This river was too deep for Tchang to walk across, the currents were too strong for him to swim across, and there was no bridge to help him cross over.

Tchang thought he was going to have to turn back home, when suddenly, from out of the river, rose a huge, long, fearsome dragon! A dragon with teeth like razors, eyes like two pools of fire and claws like daggers. A dragon with a pearl in the centre of its forehead.

14

The dragon roared, "ROOAAARRR!!!!! WHAT ARE YOU DOING ON MY RIVERBANK?"

Tchang whimpered, "I need to get to the other side; I'm going to see the great King of the West to ask him a question."

The dragon stopped and thought for a moment, then said, "I'LL TELL YOU WHAT, I'LL HELP YOU OVER TO THE OTHER SIDE IF YOU ASK HIM A QUESTION FOR ME AS WELL. I WANT YOU TO ASK HIM WHY I CAN'T FLY LIKE ALL OF THE OTHER DRAGONS."

Tchang said, "I *promise* I'll ask your question."

So the dragon made himself into a bridge and Tchang walked across to the other side of the river.

Tchang arrived at the Great King of the West's golden palace. It shone like the sun and Tchang was bathed in golden light.

He stepped inside and there he saw the Great King of the West, sitting on a golden throne.

The Great King of the West stared at Tchang and stroked his long white beard.

Eventually the King boomed, "**I know why you are here.**" His mighty voice echoed around the glorious, golden room. "**You're here to ask me questions, but know this; you may only ask me three questions, no more.**"

Tchang thought, "Well, if I ask the question for the old woman and the farmer and the dragon, then I won't be able to ask a question for myself!"

Tchang knew that he had made three promises, so he asked the questions and left.

The dragon was stomping around impatiently on the riverbank. "WHERE HAVE YOU BEEN?!" he demanded. "I'VE BEEN WAITING AGES! DID YOU ASK HIM?! DID YOU ASK THE GREAT KING OF THE WEST WHY I CAN'T FLY LIKE ALL THE OTHER DRAGONS?"

Tchang smiled and said, "Yes, I did. The Great King of the West said that you can't fly like the other dragons because you need to start doing nice things for people. Only then will he grant you your ability to fly."

The dragon stopped for a moment, thought about this, then plucked the pearl from his forehead and gave it to Tchang.

Then the dragon, once again, made himself into a bridge so that Tchang could walk across the river.

Tchang thanked the dragon and began walking. He walked and walked and walked, for forty-nine days and forty-nine nights, until at last, breathless and panting, he came to the farm. He knocked at the door.

KNOCK! KNOCK! KNOCK!

The farmer answered and said, "Tchang! You've come back to me! Did you ask my question? Did you ask the Great King of the West why my fruit trees grow no fruit?"

Tchang said, "Yes, I did. The Great King of the West said that we should dig at the roots of each of your nine fruit trees."

Tchang and the farmer began digging and underneath each of the nine fruit trees were nine boxes. When they unlocked and opened the boxes they saw that each one was filled with golden coins, shining in the sunlight.

The farmer gave Tchang one of the boxes and wished him luck on his journey.

Tchang thanked the farmer and again began to walk. He walked and walked and walked, for forty-nine days and forty-nine nights, until at last, breathless and panting, he came to the house. He knocked at the door.

KNOCK! KNOCK! KNOCK!

The old woman answered, "Tchang! You've come back to me! Thank you so much. Did you ask the Great King of the West my question? Did you ask him why my daughter speaks no words?"

Tchang said, "Yes, I did. Bring your daughter to me."

The daughter arrived and Tchang saw that she was beautiful. Very beautiful!

Tchang smiled at her and held the dragon's pearl next to her mouth. There was a flash of white light.

BRRRRING!

Suddenly, the daughter could speak! The first thing she said was, "Let's get married, Tchang!"

Tchang blushed and agreed to the wedding straight away.

After they were married, Tchang and

his new wife, and his new mother-in-law, walked. They walked and walked and walked, for forty-nine days and forty-nine nights, until at last, breathless and panting, they came to Tchang's farm. Tchang knocked at the door.

KNOCK! KNOCK! KNOCK!

When Tchang's mother answered he saw that she had gone blind because she'd cried so many tears waiting for Tchang to come home.

Tchang took the dragon's pearl, held it against her eyes and this time there were two flashes of white light.

BRRRRING!

BRRRRING!

Tchang's mother could see again!

Tchang then took the dragon's pearl and buried it on the farmland. There was a great, loud rumbling noise and suddenly lots of plants burst out of the ground. From that day on lots of things grew on Tchang's farm.

The dragon flew back to see Tchang and his family every year and brought lots and lots of presents.

Tchang and his mother and his wife and his mother-in-law all lived happily ever after.

3: Ali Baba and the Forty Thieves

(Arabian)

Once, there were two brothers, Ali Baba and Kazim Baba.

They looked completely alike but had very different personalities. Ali Baba was a poor woodcutter; he had no money at all, but he and his wife were happy. Kazim Baba was a rich merchant; he had more money than anyone else who lived in the village.

One day, Ali Baba was out chopping down a tree near the village, when he heard a noise. An evil laugh!

"BWA-HA-HA-HA!"

Ali Baba hid in the bushes and when he peeped out, there in front of him, were thieves. Many, many thieves!

"BWA-HA-HA-HA!"

The thieves laughed as they walked along the dusty track. Ali Baba started to count them . . . one . . . two . . . three . . . ten . . . twenty . . . thirty . . . forty.

Forty thieves!

"BWA-HA-HA-HA!"

The thieves were walking towards a cave, a cave that had a huge stone blocking the entrance.

The chief thief stopped the long line of looting loonies and stood in front of them.

"Now we will hide our stolen treasure, you horrible half-wits!" he growled at the other thirty-nine thieves.

The chief thief then turned to the huge stone and shouted,

"OPEN SESAME!"

The huge stone rolled to one side and the forty thieves jumped into action. They began to unload the five donkeys that walked with them, took their satchels full of stolen treasure and emptied it into the cave.

Then they came out and the chief thief shouted,

"CLOSE SESAME!"

The huge stone rolled back over the entrance of the cave. The forty thieves then skulked away laughing as they went.

"BWA-HA-HA-HA!"

Ali Baba crept up to the front of the cave; he felt the huge stone and he said the magic words,

"OPEN SESAME!"

The huge stone rolled to one side and there inside the cave was more treasure than Ali Baba could ever have imagined. There were diamonds, rubies, emeralds, pearls, sapphires and bags and bags of golden coins. Ali took two handfuls of treasure, loaded them onto his donkey and once out of the cave said,

"CLOSE SESAME!"

He then went off to find his wife, Marjiana. He told her the whole story then said, "And look Marji! I took two handfuls of golden coins with me!"

"What?!" Marji exclaimed. "But that is thieves' money! I won't spend thieves' money!"

"Ah, but my dear," smiled Ali Baba, "this money could be shared with everyone in the village! We have all been robbed so many times that I'm certain this money belongs to us anyway!"

Marji agreed, so off Ali Baba went through the village knocking on doors and sharing out the treasure with everyone. The whole village was delighted to hear Ali Baba's story and how he had successfully taken back what was once theirs. Everyone was delighted . . . except for one person. When Ali Baba went to his brother Kazim Baba's house, to give him his share of the treasure and to tell him the story, Kazim Baba said, "Are you MAD? Why didn't you fill ten donkeys' satchels with treasure? You could have been rich! Your mistake Ali; now I know the story AND the magic words, so I will take my ten donkeys to the cave."

So, Kazim Baba went off to the cave that Ali Baba had described. His ten donkeys were lined up outside as he said the magic words to the huge stone,

"OPEN SESAME!"

The huge stone then rolled open.

Kazim Baba didn't want to leave his ten donkeys outside the cave in case the thieves came back. If the thieves came back and caught him there, he'd be in trouble. So he took the donkeys inside the cave and said the magic words,

"CLOSE SESAME!"

As the stone rolled back into place, Kazim Baba turned and saw the diamonds, rubies, emeralds, pearls, sapphires and all of those golden coins. His eyes nearly popped out of his head. He whooped for joy,

"WOOOOO-HOOOOOOO!!!!"

and leapt up and down into the air.

Frantically, he began loading up the satchels on the backs of the ten donkeys. But, as he was loading them up, he got so excited that he forgot the magic word!

"Um . . . what was it again?" Kazim Baba muttered to himself. "Ummm . . . I know. . . OPEN . . . BANANAS!!! No, that's not right . . . OPEN CHICKEN NUGGETS!!! No, no, no

. . . OPEN SAUSAGES!!! Nope, er . . . OPEN PEPPERONI PIZZA!!!"

No matter how many times he tried, Kazim Baba just could not remember the magic words.

At that moment the forty thieves came back, after another successful thieving trip.

Kazim Baba suddenly heard the words,

"OPEN SESAME!"

"That's it!" cried Kazim Baba.

The huge stone rolled back and there stood the forty thieves!

When the chief thief saw Kazim Baba trying to steal their treasure he clapped his hands and forty swords were drawn. The thieves made a circle around Kazim Baba and chopped him up into tiny pieces.

"BWA-HA-HA-HA!"

The thieves laughed, but the chief thief rubbed his chin thoughtfully and said, "'Ere, somebody knew our secret hiding place and I reckon someone else might know too! I reckon this fella was from that little village down there. We should find out who this fella is. Let's go into the village, we'll ask around and find out who's gone missing. We'll find out who he is."

So, the forty thieves put on disguises.

They wore furry wigs, fake glasses, false noses, floppy beards and even funny moustaches.

"BWA-HA-HA-HA!"

They laughed as they set off to spend the day snooping around the village and talking to the people.

At the end of the day, the forty thieves met back outside the cave and, after speaking to each other, they soon discovered that it was Kazim Baba, the merchant, who had gone missing.

The chief thief said, "Let's find out if he's got any family. People always share secrets with their family. If we find

anybody who is related to him then we'll
chop them up into pieces too!"

"BWA-HA-HA-HA!"

The chief thief then chose his
sneakiest thief and sent him off into the
village to find Kazim Baba's family.

The sneaky thief spent all night peering through windows and doors looking for any family similarities. In no time, the sneaky thief looked into Ali Baba's house. He saw that Ali Baba looked identical to the man they had chopped up so the thief painted a red cross on the door of Ali Baba's house so the thieves knew which house to visit.

Now, Marji had heard someone sneaking outside their house. She saw the red cross and being a clever girl knew exactly what this meant. Marji went out with a tin of red paint and a paint brush. Then she marked everyone else's door in her street with the same red cross.

The sneaky thief went back and joined the other thieves. The band of forty then returned to the village, but when they got there, sure enough, there were red crosses all up and down the street!

The thieves were furious!

The chief thief then hatched another plan. He decided to send another spy the next night. He sent his most devious thief off into the village to find Kazim Baba's family.

The devious thief spent all night peering through windows and doors looking for any family similarities. In no time, the devious thief looked into Ali Baba's house. He saw that Ali Baba looked identical to the man they had chopped up, so the thief put a white chalk cross on the gate of Ali Baba's house in order that the thieves would know which house to visit.

Now, Marji had again heard someone sneaking outside their house. She saw the white chalk cross and again knew exactly what this meant. Marji went out with a piece of white chalk. She then marked everyone else's gate in the whole village with the same white cross.

The devious thief went back and joined

the other thieves. The band of forty then returned to the village, but again, when they got there, sure enough, there were white crosses all up and down the whole of the village!

The thieves were fuming!

The chief thief then hatched his most ruthless plan. A plan that was certain to work!

He put his disguise back on and ordered the rest of the thieves to load up a wagon with thirty-nine large jars. The thieves then tethered five donkeys to the wagon.

"Right then, I'm going to pretend to be an oil merchant and I'll pretend to be looking for Kazim Baba. I'll knock on doors and will surely be directed to his family!"

"BWA-HA-HA-HA!"

The forty thieves laughed and laughed.

"Then you lot can all hide inside the thirty-nine jars. When I give the signal, rush out and we'll chop Kazim Baba's family to pieces!"

"BWA-HA-HA-HA!"

The thirty-nine thieves then climbed inside the jars and the chief thief led the wagon down to the village calling out for Kazim Baba.

In no time at all, the people of the village told of Kazim Baba's disappearance and sent the chief thief to Ali Baba's house. The chief thief knocked at the door and when Ali Baba answered it, the chief thief said,

"Oh, boo-hoo! Boo-hoo! I've just heard about your brother! I was his dearest friend! I brought him a present of thirty-nine jars of oil and I don't know what to do! I'm so tired and hungry! Boo-hoo! Boo-hoo!"

"Oh my friend," exclaimed Ali Baba, "you must be exhausted! I don't know where my brother is, but you'd be welcome to stay at my house! Come, come inside!"

Ali Baba introduced the oil merchant to Marji and rushed off to prepare their guest a fine meal.

"How many jars of oil did you say you were giving to Kazim Baba?" asked Marji, suspiciously.

She thought about Ali Baba's encounter with the forty thieves. She thought about Kazim Baba's disappearance when looking for the treasure. She thought about the white and red crosses . . . She knew exactly what to do.

She sneaked out and tapped on the side of one of the jars, then whispered in a gruff voice, "Are you still in there?"

A voice answered back, "Yes, is it time to chop up the family inside that house yet?"

"Not yet," Marji whispered, "stay where you are." She then rushed inside, got a box of matches, and then one by one she dropped one match into each of the thirty-nine jars.

"AAARRGGHH!!! It's raining fire! AAARRGGHH!!!" The thirty-nine thieves leapt out of the jars screaming and ran away from the village, never to be seen again.

Marji then went inside to help Ali Baba cook a delicious dinner for their guest.

While the chief thief and Ali Baba were eating, Marji said, "Perhaps I should dance for you, as entertainment whilst you are eating?"

"That would be lovely!" said Ali Baba. "Thank you, Marji!"

"Yes . . . that would be lovely," said the chief thief grinning at the beautiful Marji from under his floppy beard.

Marji then began to dance. She had a long curved dagger which she waved above her head as she danced and twirled around the room. It was the most beautiful and exotic dance that Ali Baba or the chief thief had ever seen.

But in the middle of it all, Marji twirled around with the dagger and,

TTTHHHWWWWWPPPPTTTTTT!!!!!!!!!!!

plunged it into the heart of the chief thief.

"What are you doing?!" shouted Ali Baba. "You can't just stab people who come round for dinner!"

Marji peeled off the furry wig, fake glasses, false nose, floppy beard and funny moustache from the chief thief's face and Ali Baba immediately understood who it was.

He hugged his wife and thanked her for saving them. Ali Baba and his wife went back to the cave and with an

"OPEN SESAME!"

they took out all of the treasure and shared it not just with their village but with the villages all around – those where the thieves had been stealing and taking treasure.

Soon, the whole of Arabia had back what had been stolen. The country smiled and they lived happily ever after.

4: Saint George and the Dragon

(English)

Once, there lived a terrible dragon. A dragon with bright red eyes, long yellow teeth, huge fearsome claws and a thundering, deafening roar.

This dragon stomped up and down the whole of England, gobbling up anybody it met.

The King of England didn't want all of his people being eaten, so he had to come up with a plan.

He began thinking and thinking and thinking,

UNTIL . . . he had an idea!

He decided that he should put together a team of brave and handsome knights to fight against the dragon.

Knights came riding from all over the country, wearing suits of armour, carrying swords and shields. But as soon as they came close to the dragon,

SNAP!

he would gobble them all up.

So the King had to come up with another idea.

He was thinking and thinking and thinking,

UNTIL . . . he had another idea!

He decided that the dragon should be fed.

So every day, everyone in England had to give up their breakfast, their lunch and their dinner, which was fed to the ever-hungry dragon.

This worked for a while, but the people of England were starving and they were poor. Everything they had was being fed to the dragon.

Soon, the food in England began to run out.

So the King had to think of another plan!

He was thinking and thinking and
thinking,

UNTIL . . . he had another idea!

He decided that everyone in England
should draw straws and whoever drew the
shortest straw, would be taken and tied up
to the chair of sacrifice. The dragon would
gobble up whoever was there.

It was a dark and terrible time in
England. Nobody knew who would be next!
Everybody feared for their life and the lives
of their families.

Weeks passed. Eventually the King's own
daughter, the Princess, drew the short
straw!

With a sad heart, the King agreed that his daughter would be fed to the dragon.

So, the Princess was taken to the chair of sacrifice and was tied up. She waited . . . terrified.

From across the valley she saw the dragon! Its bright red eyes glistened in the sun. Its long yellow teeth dripped with saliva. Its huge fearsome claws stomped towards her. Its thundering, deafening roar echoed through the valley.

"ROOOAAARRR!!!"

The dragon came towards the Princess, getting closer and closer and closer still.

When suddenly, from over the hillside, rode a hero . . . a hero called Saint George.

As soon as Saint George saw the dragon he began galloping as fast as he could. He leapt down from his horse, pulled out his sword and let out a great and mighty battle cry,

"Raaaaaaaahhhhh!!!!!"

When the dragon heard the cry he . . . bowed to Saint George.

Saint George then untied the Princess and, using the rope, he tied a loop around the dragon's neck. Then, like a dog on a lead, Saint George took the dragon for a walk all over England, making him say sorry to anyone he'd frightened.

"**SORRY . . . SORRY . . . SORRY**," boomed the dragon.

Saint George went back to check on the Princess.

The Princess smiled and said, "Let's get married Saint George!"

But Saint George replied, "Sorry Princess . . . I have to travel off to lots of different countries rescuing people from dragons all over the world.

"BUT . . . know this . . . any time in England that you ever need my help, all you have to do is call out, *'Saint George'* and I will always be there to help you."

The Princess passed on the message right across England where we always know that Saint George will help us if ever we need it.

5: The Fire Monsters
(North American)

A long time ago, when the world was brand new, God had only just made the world, only just made the human beings and only just made the animals.

Now, human beings hadn't yet discovered fire. That was alright in the summertime when they were nice and warm but in the winter the human beings were freezing cold!

The wolf watched the human beings and felt sorry for them. He couldn't bear to see them cold and suffering, so he decided to steal them some fire.

The wolf knew that fire would keep the human beings warm. But he also knew that the fire was kept by the fire monsters. The fire monsters lived on the highest mountain in a special tent called a 'tepee'.

The wolf knew that he couldn't steal the fire from the fire monsters by himself. He knew that he would need help. So the wolf called out,

"Hoooooooowwwwwwwwwwwl!

"Who will help me?"

Just then a frog came leaping out of the pond shouting, "I'll help you, I'll help you!"

But the wolf said, "Oh Frog, you're too small to help me. I need somebody else, somebody bigger."

"Hoooooooooowwwwwwwwwwl!

"Who will help me?"

Just then a porcupine walked up and said, "I will help you Wolf!"

"Excellent!" replied the wolf,

"Hoooooooooowwwwwwwwwwl!

61

"Who else will help me?"

Just then a bear came striding along and said, "I will help you Wolf!"

"Superb!" said the wolf.

But the frog started jumping up and down going crazy saying,

"What about me? What about me? I'll help you! I'll help you!"

The wolf looked at frog, smiled and said, "Oh Frog, you're so small and green and jumpy, I don't think we need your help. I'll tell you what, you wait at the bottom of the mountain, and if we need you then we'll shout you."

The wolf turned to the porcupine and the bear and said, "When you hear me howl like this,

"Hoooooooooowwwwwwwwwl!

"Then I want you two to make this noise,

TTTWWWHHHPPPPPTTTT!"

The porcupine and the bear agreed.

Just to practise the wolf went,

"Hooooooooowwwwwwwwwl!"

and the porcupine and the bear went,

"TTTWWWHHHPPPPPTTTT!"

So, the porcupine, the bear and the
wolf went to the top of the highest
mountain. The porcupine and the bear hid
amongst the trees.

The wolf knocked at the tepee of the
fire monsters.

The fire monsters boomed,

"WHO IS THERE?"

"It's me, Wolf, please may I come in and keep warm by the fire?"

The fire monsters boomed back,

"YOU MAY COME IN!"

So the wolf went in and started warming himself by the fire. After a while, the fire monsters began to feel sleepy and they began to nod off to sleep.

As they were falling asleep, the wolf suddenly let out a loud,

"Hooooooooowwwwwwwwwl!"

and woke them up!

The porcupine and the bear heard the howl and went,

"TTTWWWHHHPPPPPTTTT!"

The fire monsters heard this and sleepily said, "What is making that silly noise?"

They then ran out of the tepee, searching for what was making the silly noise.

The wolf then stole a stick from the fire - a flaming stick.

The wolf ran out of the tepee as fast as he could and started running down the mountain. The fire monsters saw him and

they started to chase after him . . . getting
closer and closer.

The wolf knew that he would be caught so he shouted to the porcupine and threw the flaming stick over to him.

The porcupine ran as fast as he could down the mountain. The fire monsters saw him and they started to chase after him . . . getting closer and closer.

The porcupine knew that he would be caught too, so he shouted to the bear and threw the flaming stick over to him.

The bear ran as fast as he could down the mountain. The fire monsters saw him and they started to chase after him . . . getting closer and closer.

But the bear knew that he would be caught too, and just then he saw the little frog at the bottom of the mountain, so he shouted to him and threw him the flaming stick.

Frog knew that he could be caught easily by the fire monsters, but clever Frog had an idea. He put the flaming stick into his mouth and then jumped into the pond and started swimming across the water.

The fire monsters couldn't follow him because they couldn't get wet! So they went back to their tent, back to their tepee, up on the highest mountain.

The frog swam to the other side of the pond, climbed out, took the flaming stick from his mouth and walked right up to a tree.

The frog handed the flaming stick to the tree and said, "Take this and hide it."

The tree then hid the fire in its branches and Wolf gathered all the human beings together and showed them that if they were to take two branches from the tree and they were to rub them together, that is where they would find fire.

And that is how fire was hidden in every single tree, so that human beings didn't have to go cold in the winter ever again. This was all thanks to the kind wolf, all thanks to the silly noise-making porcupine and the bear, all thanks to the clever frog, but most especially all thanks to the tree.

6: January...
February
(Scottish)

There was once a cheerful old man who lived in a small village in Scotland. You couldn't meet a nicer old man than this one; he always had a kind word and a smile for everybody he met. He had worked hard his whole life and as a result his back was all hunched up on the left side. But this didn't make his mood bad.

He was often seen walking up and down the high street hunched up, waving and stopping to ask people how they were.

In this village there lived another old man. He couldn't have been any more different. This old man was the grumpiest, meanest, rudest old man you could ever meet. He too had worked hard his whole life and as a result was all hunched up on the right side. This made his mood all the worse.

He was often seen walking up and down the high street hunched up, grimacing and swearing at everyone he met.

One day, the cheerful old man was off walking down the high street and decided to go for a little stroll through the woods nearby. He often liked to stop and feed the birds and squirrels in those woods. He stopped, sat down on a fallen tree and was throwing nuts and seed around, when all of a sudden he heard strange singing coming from the trees beyond.

Singing that went,

"♫ January . . . February♫

"♫ March . . . April♫

"♫ May . . . June♫"

then again,

"♫ January . . . February♫

"♫ March . . . April♫

"♫ May . . . June♫"

and again,

"♫ January . . . February♫

"♫ March . . . April♫

"♫ May . . . June♫"

The cheerful old man thought that this
was the most beautiful singing he had ever
heard. He just couldn't help himself; he just
had to join in.

When the singing went,

"♫ January . . . February♫

"♫ March . . . April♫

"♫ May . . . June♫"

The cheerful old man went,

"♫ July . . . August♫"

At that moment, a huge green man stepped out from the trees and stood in front of the cheerful old man. The green man wasn't just wearing green, his skin was green too! And his hair, his beard, his eyes - everything! All green! The green man loomed over the cheerful old man and spoke, "Ah, thank you! Thank you so much! I've been singing that song for years and I just couldn't remember the next lines. Thank you again. It's a lovely jolly tune, isn't it?"

"Erm, yes it is!" beamed the cheerful old man.

"Is there something you want in return for helping me? Gold perhaps?" asked the green man as he pulled a mighty old box from his green trouser pocket. Gold glinted inside as the green man opened it.

"Oh, no thank you," smiled the cheerful old man. "Just seeing you happy and enjoying the song is payment enough for me."

"There must be something I can help you with!" exclaimed the green man. "What about that hunchback on your left side? I can fix that for you!"

"Ah, that would be grand! Thank you!"

With that the green man began to rub the cheerful old man's hunch.

"There you go!" boomed the green man. "Get some rest and in the morning . . . well, you'll see!"

The green man then plodded off into the woods with a smile on his face singing,

"♫ January . . . February♫

"♫ March . . . April♫

"♫ May . . . June♫

"♫ July . . . August♫"

The cheerful old man went to bed that night feeling contented that he had made someone feel happy.

In the morning, he could not believe it. He stood as straight as a tower! He'd never felt better! His hunch was completely gone from his left side.

The cheerful old man skipped out of his house and up and down the street shaking hands with everyone he met. He told his story a hundred times and everyone was overjoyed for the cheerful old man.

Everyone, except for the grumpy old man.

"You big fool!" he cried out to the

cheerful old man when he heard the story.

"I'd have taken the gold AND got my hunchback fixed too! You big fool!"

The grumpy old man then bought some nuts and seed from the local store and hobbled off into the woods.

The grumpy old man started to throw the nuts and seed at any animal he saw. Soon enough, all of the woodland animals had scattered and hid, afraid of being pelted with food.

Then, all was quiet and still in the wood. The grumpy old man sat down and listened.

"♫ January . . . February♫

"♫ March . . . April♫

"♫ May . . . June♫

"♫ July . . . August♫"

The grumpy old man then called out,

"September, October, November and you forgot about December as well, you great green goony!"

The green man stepped out from the woods. The grumpy old man really hadn't expected him to be so large!

He gulped and said, "Erm, so I helped you with your song, like. So, erm, can I have some gold then or what?"

The green man frowned, reached into his green trouser pocket and pulled out the mighty old box. He threw it over to the grumpy old man and knocked him off his feet.

But the grumpy old man didn't mind. He grinned as he greedily opened the box and stared at the golden coins inside.

The green man then turned to walk off into the woods when the grumpy old man called out, "Hey! Wait on, you big dafty! What about me old hunchback, eh? What about fixing that, too?!"

The green man stomped over and roughly rubbed at the grumpy old man's back, then said, "Get some rest. Then in the morning . . . you'll see."

He then walked off into the woods singing,

"♫ January . . . February♫

"♫ March . . . April♫

"♫ May . . . June♫

"♫ July . . . August♫

"♫ September . . . October♫

"♫ November . . . December♫"

The grumpy old man went to bed that night feeling very excited. He put the mighty old box on the floor next to his bed and slipped into peaceful sleep.

His first thoughts in the morning were of his hunch. He pulled himself out of bed and to his horror, discovered that his hunch was still there. And, even worse . . . now he had one on the left side too!

The grumpy old man kicked the mighty old box in temper. The lid swung open and there, inside, were no longer golden coins, but instead was dust!

"WHAT?!" bellowed the grumpy old man, "I've been tricked!"

The grumpy old man then stomped out of the house and into the woods shouting insults and swearing terribly, searching for the green man.

The grumpy old man was never seen again.

And if you go into the woods, and you hear strange singing, then watch out! Because the green man rewards those who do good . . . and may just punish those who do not!

7: The Tree of Knowledge

(Jewish)

Mendel the Fool was begging from
village to village, town to town, city to city.

What little money he got he spent on
expensive food and wine. He had tried lots
of jobs but nobody wanted a fool working
for them.

One day, Mendel was walking the length of a long, dusty track when suddenly, a huge storm raged in the sky. The wind howled and the rain burst from the clouds. Everything was swept up into the air. Mendel grabbed a large rock and held on tight. The wind and the rain swirled all around but still he kept his grip. Even a fool knows when his life is in danger!

After many minutes had passed the storm disappeared as quickly as it had appeared.

Mendel let go of the rock. Everything became clear. Not just in the sky, but in Mendel's mind. He understood the way of the world. How it was all intricately balanced. He understood the language of the birds around him. Mendel smiled and, lost in new thoughts, wandered to the nearest town.

In the market place he found a group of wise men deep in debate. Mendel answered the questions they had discussed all day long. He solved riddles that people posed to him. He settled disputes. He solved arguments.

The people were amazed! Was this the same Mendel they had seen begging earlier? The same fool who needed help to do up his sandals?

Mendel was given coin after coin for his ability to solve problems and for his wisdom.

Mendel used his money to find food and shelter in a tavern. He asked for a hot bath to be prepared as the storm had left him dusty and dirty.

Mendel took off his robes and his sandals and as quickly as he had become wise, he suddenly became foolish again.

He slipped on a bar of soap and fell head first into the bath.

Once clean, Mendel put his old robes and dirty sandals back on; he instantly became wise again!

What *wise* Mendel thought was that the source of his wisdom was his robes. What he didn't realise was that during the storm, a leaf from the Tree of Knowledge had blown all the way from the Garden of Eden and had wedged itself into one of his sandals. This was the source of his wisdom!

Mendel became famous across the land. People travelled for miles to hear his lessons and his ability to debate with anyone.

Eventually, news of Mendel's wisdom reached the King. The King sent his messenger and summoned Mendel to his court.

"Ah, there you are Mendel the Wise," smiled the King when Mendel arrived. "My daughter has been struck blind as a result of a fever she caught. All of the doctors in the land have tried to heal her . . . all have failed. Can you, wise Mendel, help my daughter?"

"I will try, Your Majesty," answered Mendel.

Once Mendel saw the King's daughter he instantly fell in love. She was the most beautiful girl he had ever seen.

Mendel opened her closed eyes and knew at once what to do.

He went straight to a fig tree that grew outside of the King's palace and collected some of the sap, bark and leaves. Then Mendel used a pestle and mortar to grind the ingredients into a lotion. He then rubbed the lotion onto the Princess' eyes - and she could see!

The King was overjoyed. He made Mendel his chief advisor straight away.

Several months passed. The King ruled more wisely than ever with Mendel at his side. But each day the King questioned Mendel about the source of his knowledge.

Each day Mendel would reply with the same
answer,

"It's my robes and my sandals, Your
Majesty!"

"Those dirty old things!" the King would
laugh. "Those are the robes of a beggar!
Come now, Mendel; tell me the truth!"

Each day would be the same until
eventually the King relented and said, "Very
well, Mendel the Wise. I believe you. It is
your robes and your sandals that bring you
great knowledge. After all, you never change
them! What price do you ask for me to buy
them off you?"

"I don't want to sell them. Sorry, Your

Majesty," Mendel replied.

"How about one bag of gold?!" asked the King.

Each day the King would offer Mendel a new price and each day he would refuse.

"Two bags of gold . . . Three then! Four! Ten!!!" the King would say.

"I'm sorry," is all Mendel would reply.

But one day, the King made Mendel an offer he could not refuse.

"Very well, Mendel the Wise," said the King, "I offer you half of my kingdom for your robes and your sandals."

"I don't want to sell them. Sorry, Your Majesty," Mendel replied.

The King nodded and said, "Half my kingdom . . . and my daughter's hand in marriage."

Mendel agreed, overjoyed to marry the girl he had loved since the moment he had first seen her.

Mendel gave up his dusty old robes and dirty sandals and changed into luxurious felt clothes and soft leather shoes. He also changed back into a fool.

The King held the robes and sandals in his hands and pulled a face. He couldn't bear to wear them as they were.

"Go and have these cleaned and washed, then bring them straight back to me!" the King ordered his servants.

The robes were washed and the sandals were cleaned.

When the King wore Mendel's washed robes and cleaned sandals he felt no different. The leaf from the Tree of Knowledge had been washed away. He never did admit to anyone he had given up half his kingdom and his daughter for nothing. So no-one found out the secret.

As for Mendel and the Princess? They were married and she ruled their half of the kingdom wisely enough for both of them. Mendel may have been a fool again . . . but he was a happy fool. They lived happily ever after.

8: William and the Witch

(English)

William was a naughty boy. He never listened to his teachers, he didn't listen to his parents, and he didn't even listen to his friends. One day, while William was playing football in the school yard, his teacher said to him, "William, you shouldn't play so roughly, you shouldn't be fouling everybody! Whenever you play football we get nothing but complaints and pretty soon no one's going to want to play with you."

William didn't listen. He went off playing football and fouled everybody, knocked them left, right and centre. Of course, after a while nobody wanted to play football with William any more!

Another time, William's parents said to him, "William, don't climb that tree in the garden any more, the branches are all rotten. If you climb up there you might fall and hurt yourself."

William didn't listen to them. He climbed up into the tree, the branches snapped and he fell down and broke his arm!

After his arm had healed, William was out playing on the beach with his friends. They decided to go rock pooling. William ran across the smooth black rocks as fast as he could.

His friends said to him, "You know what, William, you'd better be careful running across those rocks, they're really slippery!"

William didn't listen; he continued to run as fast as he could, slipped over and . . . he broke the same arm again!

Now, William's teachers and his parents AND his friends always told him never, ever, ever, EVER to play outside in the streets at night. Everybody knew that a witch lived in William's village and everybody knew she liked eating little boys more than anything else! William didn't listen to them. He went out to play every night. Usually he returned home before it got dark. But on one particular night William was distracted.

No one wanted to play football with him, so William kicked the ball up and down the streets on his own looking for someone to play with. He hadn't noticed that it had become dark. Very dark.

Suddenly William heard,

"HA HA HA HA HAAAAAAAAAAA!!!!!"

It was a hideous witch's cackle.

He stopped, picked up his football and

listened again,

"HA HA HA HA HAAAAAAAAAAAA!!!!!"

William thought to himself, "That sounds like a very jolly lady! I wonder if she'd like to play football with me."

So he listened carefully once more and heard the

"HA HA HA HA HAAAAAAAAAAAA!!!!!"

William realised it was coming from a cottage, down at the far side of the village. He walked towards it and saw that smoke was bellowing out of the chimney. He went up and knocked at the door. The door opened and there stood a hideous witch. She had a long pointed nose that was covered in warts. She had big bushy eyebrows, bright yellow eyes and green, warty skin.

Her huge spiky hair was covered in head lice that wriggled and jiggled around her head.

The witch grinned a hideous smile and screeched, *"Hello there little boy, mmm . . . you look good enough to eat. Come in!"*

The witch then dragged William inside her cottage. She hooked a cauldron above the fire, poured in a huge jug of water, turned round and smiled her terrible smile.

"I think I'll be having boiled boy for my supper tonight!"

"Oh, erm, sorry, but I'm going to have to be off," said William as he backed towards the door. He turned to run through it but the witch's huge black dog blocked his way. It had bright red eyes and matted fur and it growled at William.

"GGRRRRRRRR!!!!"

William thought as quickly as he could and suddenly he had an idea. "Ewwww! Don't have boiled boy! Boiled boy's not very nice, my granny told me. She reckons that boy pie is much nicer!"

"*Boy pie?*" screeched the witch, "*I can't be bothered with all that, I can't be bothered to make pastry!*"

"Well, you can get ready-made pastry now, you know. You just have to fly off to your local supermarket; I think there's one down the road."

"*Oh really?*"

"Yes, you get yourself off and I'll wait here," smiled William.

"*Oh lovely, I'll be back in a minute,*" said

the witch as she flew off to the supermarket on her broomstick.

William then looked at the witch's black dog and looked at the football under his arm.

He smiled and began to bounce the ball.

The dog's eyes followed it.

Up and down. Up and down.

William threw the ball to one side of the room and the dog chased after it, collected the ball and enthusiastically brought it back.

William did it again.

Up and down. Up and down.

Then he threw it to the other side of the room. The dog ran after it and fetched it back.

William then opened the door and threw the ball as far as he could and the dog went running after it.

William then picked up a poker from the fire and hid behind the door. When the dog came back,

CLUNK!

he bashed the dog on the head and the dog flopped down to the ground, unconscious.

William ran out of the house as quickly as he could; he ran past houses, past street lamps, past post boxes and down onto the beach. He could see his home beyond the smooth black rocks and ran faster than ever.

But just then the witch was flying home carrying her shopping bag. She saw William escaping, landed on the beach and chased after him on all fours, like a dog!

William ran faster and faster and faster over the rocks but then he remembered what his friends had told him - that he should never run over the slippery black rocks by the beach. So he stopped and stepped carefully over the rocks. One foot at a time, slowly does it.

The witch came running faster and faster and faster and she . . . slipped on the rocks and plunged into the sea! The waves pulled her in and she was never seen again.

From that day on, William always listened to his teachers, he always listened to his parents and he always listened to his friends . . . well, when they were talking sense anyway!

Also available from

PUBLISHING

Snakes' Legs and Cows' Eggs by Adam Bushnell
ISBN 978-1-905637-21-8
Selected for the SLA Boys into Books (5-11) 2008 List

Donkeys' Wings and Worms' Stings by Adam Bushnell
ISBN 978-1-905637-50-8

What happens when you sneeze with your eyes open? When a woodcutter meets a dragon? When a giant wants a new slave? Or when fire monsters try to keep the world feeling icy?
The two books above by Adam Bushnell include traditional tales and brand new stories, each told with serious silliness. Each book is comprised of eight stories which bring together characters from all over the world.

A Marrow Escape by Stephanie Baudet
ISBN 978-1-900818-82-7

Dad has flu and it's Kelly's job to look after his prize marrow. But when it goes missing she needs to work hard to stop him from finding out. Can she get the prize veggie back in time for the big competition on Saturday? With the help of her brother Zac and his friends, the chase is on...

The One That Got Away by Stephanie Baudet
ISBN 978-1-900818-87-2

When Mike and Sophie have the idea of looking after small pets while their owners are on holiday, they think it will be an easy way of making some pocket money. But some of the pets are not quite what they had bargained for. And when one of them escapes, there's no telling where it will end up...

The Mum Manager by Suzi Cresswell
ISBN 978-1-905637-45-4

Toby plays for a successful football team. But there's a problem: the manager is leaving the area and Toby's mum, Sharon, a hairdresser and yoga teacher, is the only volunteer to take on the role. Will she be up to the challenge? Toby doubts it as the first training session involves yoga, dance routines and lots of chatting...

Porky Pies by Suzi Cresswell
ISBN 978-1-905637-66-9

Jaz has a bad habit - he can't stop telling little white lies. When he joins a new school, he tells his classmates that he's the son of pop star Rocky Riff. Jaz finds himself in big trouble when Aisha turns out to be Rocky's greatest fan and Clint demands proof...

Jade Fry, Private Eye by Suzi Cresswell
ISBN 978-1-905637-75-1

Jade is fed up when she has to stay with her Gran. But life there is more exciting than expected as she is soon swept up in an exciting adventure involving Gran's pony, Captain. Captain is important to Gran's friend, a race horse trainer whose star horse, Smithy, is due to run in the Melton Chase soon. Without Captain, Smithy won't get into the horse box. But it seems that someone wants to stop him competing when Captain disappears. Jade turns detective and follows the trail to find out what is going on...

Skateboard Gran by Ian MacDonald
ISBN 978-1-905637-30-0

Tom is very sensible; his Gran, on the other hand, is completely bonkers! When Tom finds himself in a spot of financial bother, the prize in a skateboard competition seems to be the answer. The only problem is that he is too scared to skateboard! He is delighted when Gran offers to enter the competition, until she has an accident on her board. Then Tom has to face his own fears...and ride the terrifying 'Wall of Death'...

Chip McGraw by Ian MacDonald
ISBN 978-1-905637-08-9

Chip McGraw is the toughest cowboy in the West. He drinks lemonade from a dirty glass...and he doesn't even carry a gun. Bradley McIntire has two heroes in his life: his dad and Chip McGraw. But when burglars turn up at the school disco, is it Dad or Chip McGraw who saves the day?

Trevor's Trousers by David Webb
ISBN 978-1-904904-19-9

How can a pair of trousers cause so much trouble? When Trevor promises to look after his new school trousers, it proves an impossible task. A priceless ruby ring, blundering thieves and a trip to the town tip can only lead to disaster! Poor Trevor! At least there is a reward waiting for him at the end of the adventure...

Friday the Thirteenth by David Webb
ISBN 978-1-905637-37-9

On Friday the thirteenth, Callum has to walk to school in the freezing cold, as he's been held up by his annoying sister. Things go from bad to worse when Callum arrives at school late to face Mr Wiggins, his strict teacher who makes him look after the dreadful Daisy, a new girl at school. However, Callum rises to the challenge when the school computers are stolen and Friday the thirteenth turns into his lucky day!

The Library Ghost by David Webb
ISBN 978-1-904374-66-4

It's Victorian Day at Mill Street School to help raise money for a new library! Children and staff are all dressed up in Victorian costume. All except for the sneering spoilsport, Delia Grime, that is. All goes well until Delia causes chaos at the coffee afternoon, trying to kidnap a valuable Victorian china doll. However, she's in for a ghostly shock when she makes her escape to the old school library!

Dinosaur Day by David Webb
ISBN 978-1-904374-67-1

It's Dinosaur Day and Terri Timpson is really excited. However, her class trip to the dinosaur exhibition at the museum provides far more excitement than she bargained for! Cunning thieves plan to steal the priceless Stone of Methesda from the Egyptian Gallery - until Terri and her friends leap into action! An exciting and hilarious adventure, that will keep its readers gripped to the end...

Grandma's teeth by David Webb
ISBN 978-1-905637-20-1

Dudley Drummond's half term is ruined when his awful grandma comes to stay. Things go from bad to worse when she loses not one but two sets of false teeth! The story moves at a fast pace, with a trip to the dentist, a disastrous bus journey and a run in with local vandals...

The Bears Bite Back by Derek Keilty
ISBN 978-1-905637-36-2

This is a humorous and wacky sequel to *Goldilocks and the Three Bears*. The three bears are fuming after the ringleted prowler has left their place in disarray. They quickly decide to get their own back by following the intruder's footprints and marching over to her house to eat her food, break her furniture and sleep in her bed!

Magic Beans on Toast by Derek Keilty
ISBN 978-1-905637-58-4

Zoe plants a magic bean and is soon scaling an enormous beanstalk to Giant Land, where she is captured by the grandsons of the Giant from *Jack and the Beanstalk*...

Order online @ **www.eprint.co.uk**